Abilene's Cloudy Journey

A tale of a cloud and courage

DR. FERDIE CADET

Illustrations by Blueberry Illustrations

Copyright © 2021 by Dr. Ferdie Cadet

All rights reserved.

No part of this book may be reproduced or transmitted in any form or by any means without written permission from the author.

ISBN: 978-0-578-99784-1

For my nephews Fabyan, Nathan, Alexander, Kealyn, and Christopher and my nieces Charnyl and Shelby. May you always find the cOUrage to stand your grOUnd against all odds.

To Maggie for living with cOUrage and seizing each moment.

To my dream Giver for the missed opportunities, the rejections, the inconveniences, and all the sleepless nights as I embrace them as an opportunity to create and give birth to Abilene.

This morning, she has no idea that she is abOUt to face Hazy, the mean clOUd on the bus.

The school bus comes on time. Abilene gets on the bus withOUt knowing that today is the day that she gets hOUnded.

As usual, Abilene sits in the back by the window so that she can freely daydream. She thinks abOUt her science project.

She had learned that there are more than a hundred types of clOUds that are grOUped based on their shape and height. She memorized all of the different types and their names.

She knows that cumulus clOUds look like snowflakes, while nimbostratus clOUds are the thick ones when rain falls. She wonders which one Hazy is today.

Today, Hazy enters the bus with her friends who flOUt at the children withOUt grOUnds. Abilene is used to all the hullabaloo.

Suddenly, a clOUd of uncertainty hangs over her as she sees Hazy and her friends approaching her.

Abilene is abOUt to face a clOUd that she had never faced before. You see, on many occasions, Hazy comes up with different games and she bullies the other children on the bus with different bets.

She tries to distract herself and so she pulls OUt one of her books from her bag.

Hazy asks her to get up from her seat. Abilene just shakes her head.

She does her best to stay calm.
But deep inside, she shakes with fear.

Hazy asks again, but this time she pulls Abilene.

At the cOUnt of 15, Hazy let go. She seems to give up, as she is unable to pull Abilene away from her seat.

**Hazy's friends decide to give it a go.
They come forward and start pulling Abilene with more force.**

Abilene wants to cry. She hopes someone will vOUch for her. But nothing. No one does. She then begins to imagine the sun shining thrOUgh and the cirrostratus clOUds rushing to her rescue.

Abilene visualizes her bullies as clOUds. She repeats lOUdly this time, "cU-mU-lUs, stra-tUs, cU-mU-lUs, stra-to-cU-mU-lUs," and wishes they wOUld just disappear into thin air!

Suddenly, she hears several shOUts. The school bus driver and the other children on the bus all start shOUting, "cU-mU-lUs, stra-tUs, cU-mU-lUs, stra-to-cU-mU-lUs."

Hazy and her friends get so puzzled that
they silently go back to their seats
and do not utter a single word.

Abilene gets OUt of the bus and lifts her head toward the sky. She sees her favorite clOUd, the cirrus. She tries to suppress a giggle. For Abilene, cirrus represents the calm before the storm.

**Abilene is not living in a clOUd cuckoo land.
She realizes she just won one of her battles.**

Dr. Ferdie Cadet has worked closely with diverse populations, offering clinical interventions and behavioral management services to at-risk students. As an educator, she has conducted many international comparative research studies. She recognizes the significant impact in the worlds of education, mental health, leadership, and community development that address the most pressing problems for our future generation. She takes great pride and joy in serving and making a positive impact in children's lives. She will continue to write books that help kids unleash their inner superheroes...

CPSIA information can be obtained
at www.ICGtesting.com
Printed in the USA
BVHW021000220222
629764BV00005B/216